Big Spring Clean

One morning, Looby Loo was having a big spring clean, and Andy Pandy and Teddy were helping. Teddy was enjoying mopping so much, he even mopped the bed.

Looby Loo said that her bed didn't need mopping.

Then Teddy accidentally knocked a painting of Looby Loo with his wet mop.

The painting was ruined. Looby Loo told Teddy he should have been more careful. It was his fault.

Teddy said he'd only been trying to help.
He stormed out, slamming the door behind him.

Soon, Andy Pandy and Looby Loo had finished the cleaning, and Andy Pandy said goodbye. As Andy Pandy was walking home he met Bilbo. Bilbo asked Andy Pandy if he could help Bilbo clean his boathouse, too.

Bilbo's boathouse hadn't been cleaned for a long time. It was dusty, and it made Andy Pandy sneeze. "Ahhh-tisssh-ooo!"

Andy Pandy sneezed so hard he fell onto Bilbo's collection of seashells, and knocked them all over the ground.

Andy Pandy had an idea. He asked Bilbo if he could have some of the seashells, and some bits of rope and seaweed.

Bilbo wondered what Andy Pandy wanted them for.
After Andy Pandy had explained, Bilbo was happy to
let him have what he wanted.

Andy Pandy took the seashells, rope and seaweed to Teddy's house.

He found some cardboard, glue, brushes and paints. Then he explained to Teddy that they were going to make a picture of Looby Loo to replace the painting Teddy had spoilt.

Andy Pandy showed
Teddy how to make
a picture by sticking
the shells, rope and
seaweed onto the
card. At first, Teddy
found it quite tricky...

...but he soon got the hang of it.

Once Teddy had finished sticking things, it was
time to finish the picture using paint.

Teddy was very pleased with the picture when it was finished. Andy Pandy told Teddy he should give it to Looby Loo, to say he was sorry for spoiling her painting.

Teddy was afraid that Looby Loo might still be cross with him, but Andy Pandy said he had to be brave.

Teddy told Looby Loo that he'd come to say he was
sorry for what had happened to her painting earlier.
He'd made her a picture to replace it.

He hoped she liked it.

Looby Loo was very pleased. She thanked Teddy and Andy Pandy very much for the lovely picture, and invited them both in for a special tea.